BEACH DAY!

Patricia Lakin
pictures by Scott Nash

DIAL BOOKS FOR YOUNG READERS

For my mom, Eva Koretsky Lakin,
who knew the joys to be found at the beach
—P.L.

To SW and NGN
I couldn't have done it without you
—S.N.

Published by Dial Books for Young Readers
A division of Penguin Young Readers Group
345 Hudson Street
New York, New York 10014
Text copyright © 2004 by Patricia Lakin
Pictures copyright © 2004 by Scott Nash
All rights reserved
Designed by Kimi Weart
Text set in Gill Sans
Manufactured in China on acid-free paper

1 3 5 7 9 10 8 6 4 2

Library of Congress Cataloging-in-Publication Data
Lakin, Patricia, date.
Beach day! / Patricia Lakin ; pictures by Scott Nash.
p. cm.
Summary: Four friends have many adventures on the way to the beach.
ISBN 0-8037-2894-8
[1. Beaches—Fiction. 2. Friendship—Fiction.]
I. Nash, Scott, date, ill. II. Title.
PZ7.L1586 Be 2004
[E]—dc21
2002153146

The illustrations were created using gouache and pencil.

“SUNNY,”
said Pam.

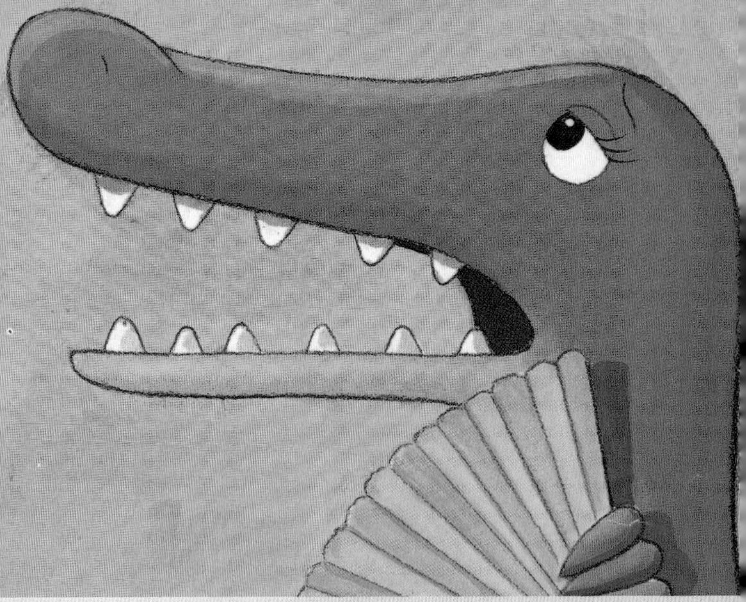

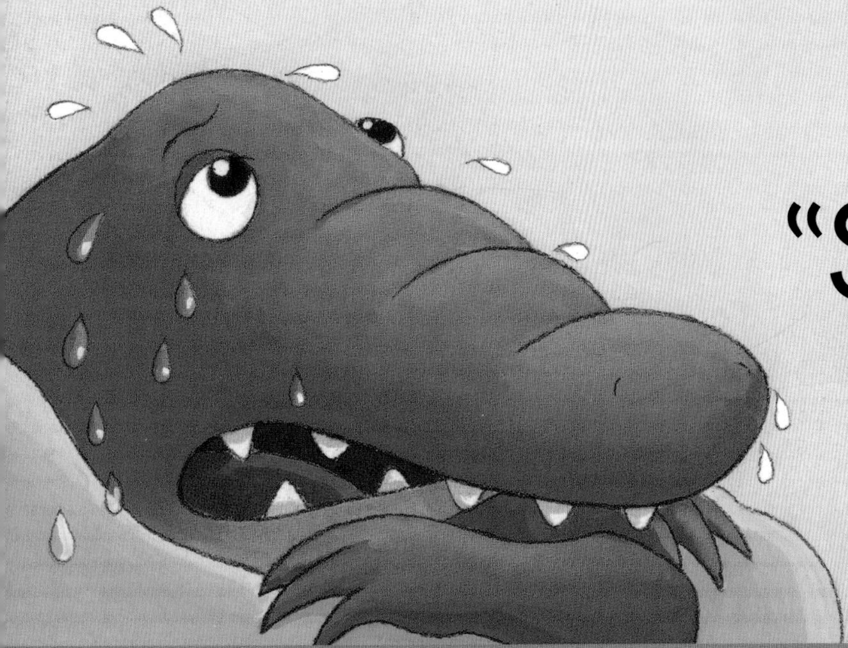

“SWEATY,”
said Will.

“SWIM?”
said Jill.

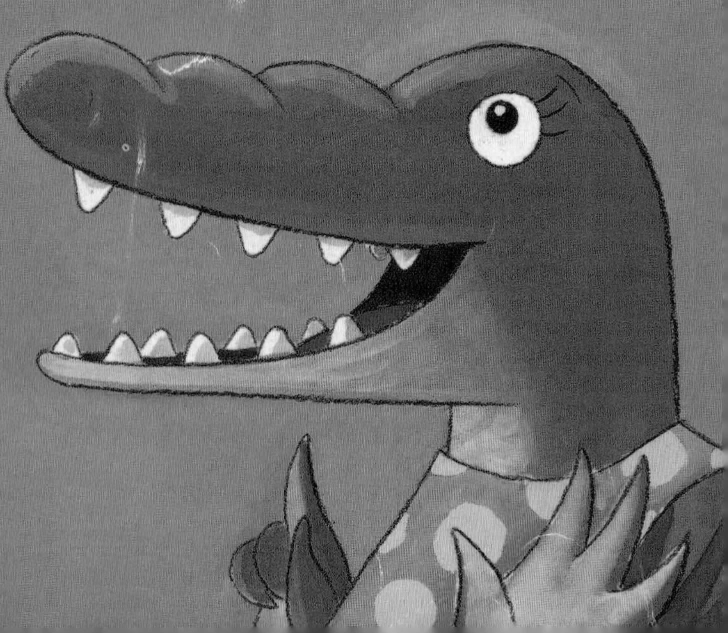

"BEACH!"

said Sam, Pam,
Will and Jill.

"Swimsuits,"
said Sam.

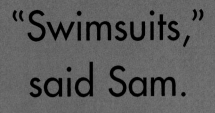

"Sun hats,"
said Pam.

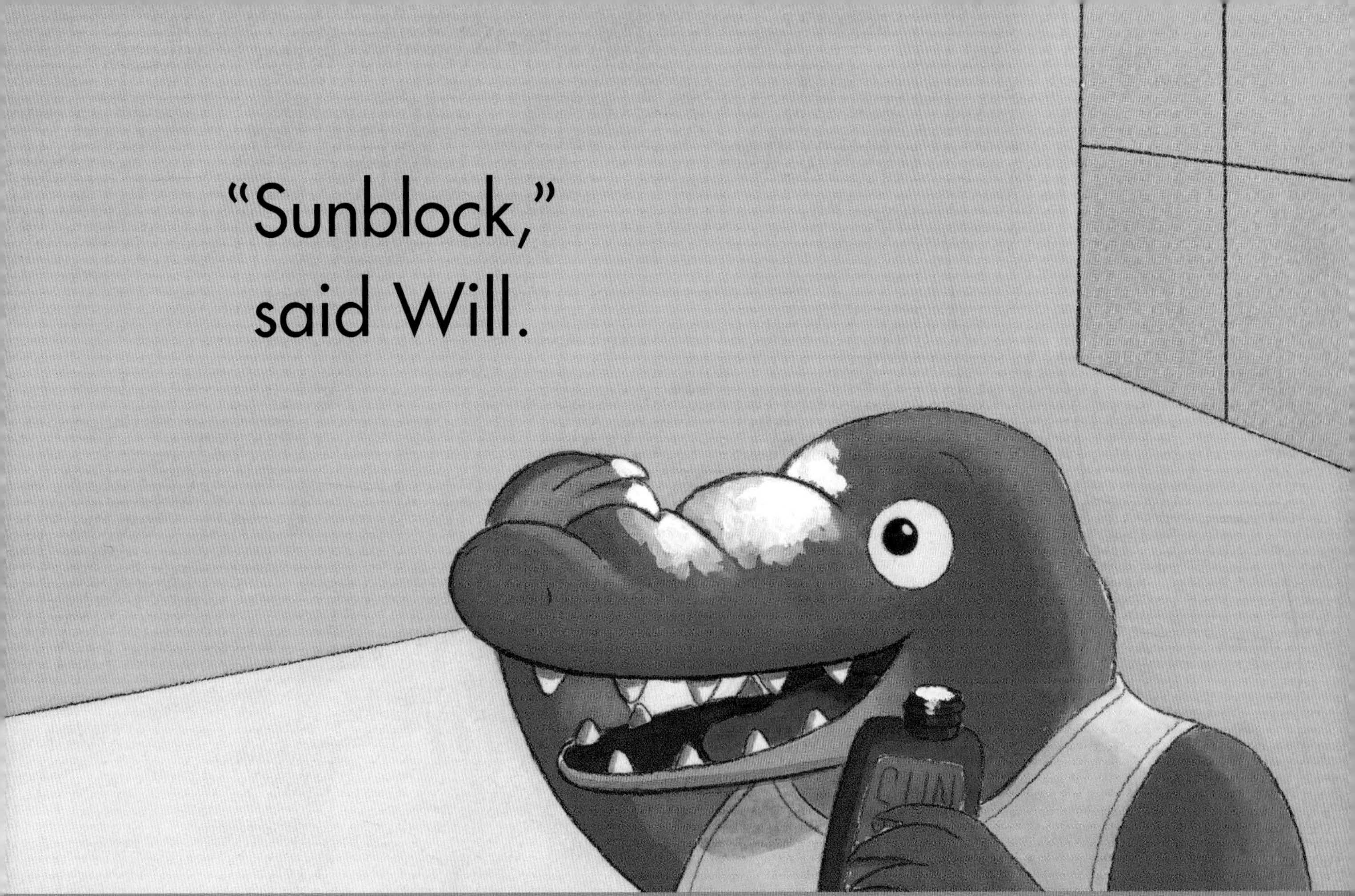

"Sunblock,"
said Will.

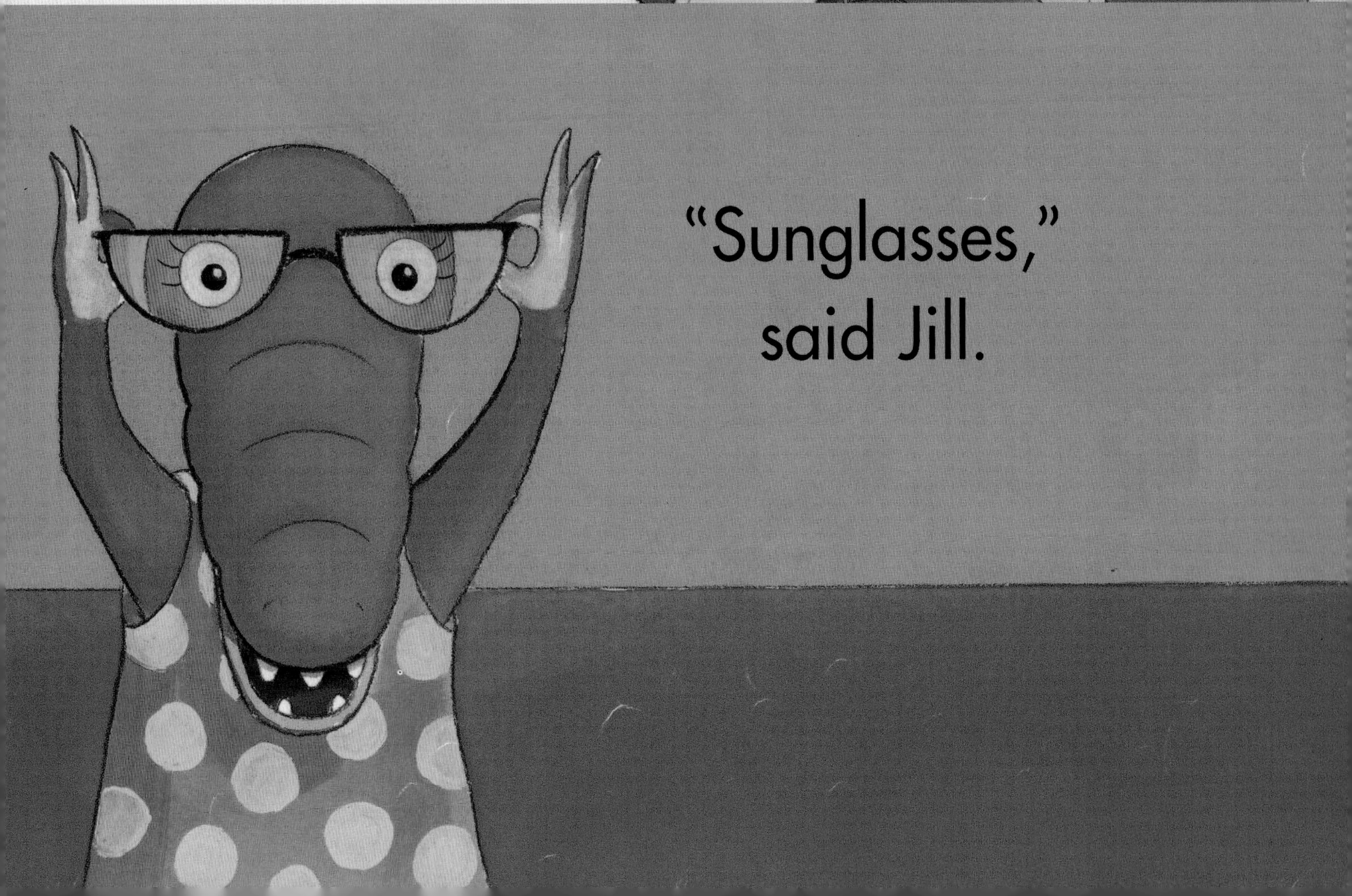

"Sunglasses,"
said Jill.

"WE'RE

said Sam, Pam,

OFF!"

Will and Jill.

"LOOK!"
said Sam.

"A park!" said Pam.
"With swings," said Will.
"And slides," said Jill.

PLAY!"

said
Sam,
Pam,
Will
and
Jill.

"Left,"
said Will.

"Right,"
said Jill.

sighed Sam, Pam, Will and Jill.

They pedaled
UP.

They pedaled
DOWN.

They looked for beach signs all around.

They pedaled
UNDER.

They pedaled
OVER.

They
pedaled
in

a field
of clover.

"PICNIC!"

said Sam, Pam, Will and Jill.

"Sandwich,"
said Sam.

"Pasta,"
said Pam.

"Pickles,"
said Will.

"BURP!"
said Jill.

"NAP TIME,"

said Sam, Pam, Will and Jill.

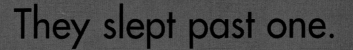

They slept past one.

They slept past two.

They slept past three.

They slept past four.

"Let's go!"
said Sam.

"But where?"
said Pam.

"Over there!"
said Will.

"That hill?"
said Jill.

BEACH

"PUSH!"

said Sam, Pam, Will and Jill.

"Sand," said Sam.
"Water," said Pam.
"Waves," said Will.
"Gulls," said Jill.

"BEACH!"

said Sam, Pam, Will and Jill.

"No umbrellas," said Sam.
"No snack bar," said Pam.
"No chairs," said Will.
"No people," said Jill.

"NO SUN!"

cried Sam, Pam, Will and Jill.

Sam, Pam, Will and Jill looked up.

Then Sam, Pam, Will and Jill smiled.

And they swam by the light
of the moon.